THE
FAVERSHAMS
ROY GERRARD

GOLLANCZ CHILDREN'S PAPERBACKS
LONDON

One day in eighteen fifty-one
These parents posed beside their son.
The son (that's him inside the pram)
Was Charles Augustus Faversham,
And now this book relates the life
Of Charles Augustus and his wife.

At school young Charles did very well
And quickly learnt to read and spell.
He earned himself the teachers' praise
With addings-up and take-aways.
At work or sport he did his best
And seemed to rise above the rest.

"FEAR GOD
HONOUR THE QUEEN
SHOOT STRAIGHT
AND KEEP CLEAN"

DIGNITY   BRAVERY   KINDNESS

Next, in the army Charles appeared
(Well, fancy that, he's grown a beard)
And though he did not like to shout
Or order other men about
He served his Queen and did his bit
And kept the soldiers smart and fit.

And when the regiment was sent
To teach our foes what justice meant
He showed his men how to behave
By being very strong and brave
Though badly wounded in the knee –
Major Faversham, V.C.

Back home, he tried to cure his knee
By exercising constantly
And thus, whilst on a cycle ride,
He came across his future bride.
They rode together for a spell
And found they got on very well.

Charles and his friend, Amelia Gwen,
Soon arranged to meet again,
And so they did, and found that they
Were meeting almost every day.
Their friendship slowly turned to love
And they got married (see above).

Their honeymoon was several weeks
In Switzerland, among the peaks.
Charles thought it absolutely bliss
To climb a mighty precipice.
Gwen secretly was out of breath
And rather hot and scared to death.

On their return Charles got this letter,
'Dear Sir, now that your leg is better,
Kindly take your troops and sail
For India, Wednesday, without fail.'
They sat and wondered what to do,
And Gwen said she was going, too.

In India they found that life
Was very nice for man and wife,
And each day when their work was done
They spent the evenings having fun
With picnics, games and social calls
And jolly regimental balls.

Charles took some time off for a while
To shoot a wicked crocodile
Which chewed up people by the score.
(They say it swallowed ninety-four.)
And all those who had not been chewed
Came round to show their gratitude.

Gerrard

And then, to their eternal joy,
Gwen had a bouncing baby boy,
And two years later it befell
She had a little girl as well.
Charles left the army, for his plan
Was to become a family man.

They bought a house in Gloucestershire
And there they lived for many a year
Content as anyone could please
Among the spacious lawns and trees,
With lots of servants, maids and cooks,
For Charles made money writing books.

The family loved to walk for hours
Among the hedgerows and the flowers,
But Charles would often find that he
Had trouble with his wounded knee;
And when he did, with loving care,
Gwen pushed him in an old wheel-chair.

The children often stayed with friends
Or relatives, for long weekends,
Then Charles and Gwen would slip away
To bathe in some secluded bay.
(I hope that you won't think it rude
To show them paddling in the nude.)

The years went by, the children grew.
In time they both got married too,
But as they lived not far away
They'd bring their families to stay.
Observe them here, on this last page,
With Charles and Gwen in their old age.

First published in Great Britain 1982
by Victor Gollancz Ltd

First Gollancz Children's Paperbacks edition 1993
by Victor Gollancz
A Cassell imprint
Villiers House, 41/47 Strand, London WC2N 5JE

A catalogue record for this book is
available from the British Library

ISBN 0 575 05660 6

Printed and bound in Hong Kong
by Dah Hua Printing Co.